E HOWE
Brontorina /

35000097230444

Brontorina

JAMES HOWE

illustrated by RANDY CECIL

CANDLEWICK PRESS

First paperback edition 2013

The Library of Congress has cataloged the hardcover edition as follows:

Howe, James, date.
Brontorina / by James Howe ; illustrated by Randy Cecil. —1st ed.
p. cm.
Summary: Despite her size and not having the proper footwear, a determined dinosaur pursues
her dream of becoming a ballerina.
ISBN 978-0-7636-4437-6 (hardcover)
[1. Dinosaurs—Fiction. 2. Ballet dancing—Fiction. 3. Size—Fiction.] I. Cecil, Randy, ill. II. Title.
PZ7.H83727Br 2010
[E]—dc22   2009038052

ISBN 978-0-7636-5323-1 (paperback)

17 LEO 10

Printed in Heshan, Guangdong, China

This book was typeset in Wilke Bold.
The illustrations were done in oil.

Candlewick Press
99 Dover Street
Somerville, Massachusetts 02144

visit us at www.candlewick.com

For Mark, a dancer in his heart

J. H.

For Sophie

R. C.

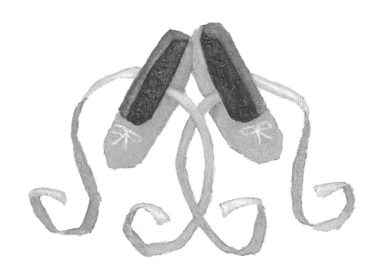

Brontorina had a dream.

"But you are a dinosaur," Madame Lucille
pointed out.

"True," Brontorina replied. "But in my heart
I am a ballerina."

Madame Lucille wondered what to do. She had
never had a dinosaur as a student before. Dinosaurs
were rather large. And this one certainly did not
have the right shoes.

But then she felt Clara and Jack tugging at her
skirt. "Oh, please!" they pleaded.

Madame Lucille looked into the dinosaur's eyes. "What is your name, my dear?"

"Brontorina. Brontorina Apatosaurus. I even sound like a dancer, don't you agree?"

Madame Lucille did agree. How could she not?

"Welcome to Madame Lucille's Dance Academy for Girls and Boys," she said. "Please try not to squash the other dancers.

"Music, Magnolia!" she commanded the piano player.

As Magnolia began to play, Madame Lucille turned her commands to her students.

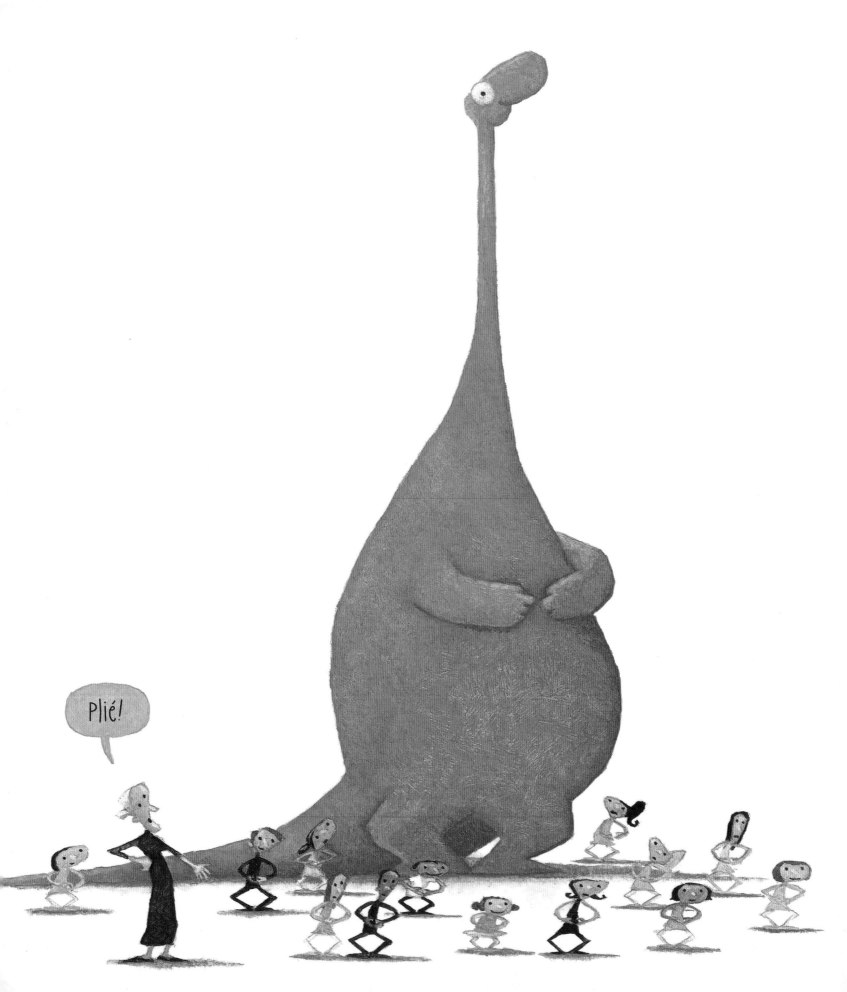

"What a graceful dancer you are, my dear!" Madame Lucille exclaimed.

Brontorina blushed. "On the outside, I am a dinosaur. But in my heart—"

"You are a ballerina!" cried Clara and Jack.

She still doesn't have the right shoes!

In the weeks that followed . . .

"Oh, Brontorina!" cried Madame Lucille. "I'm afraid you are too big to be a ballerina. You barely fit in my studio. And how in the world will a male dancer ever lift you over his head?"

"I could do it!" Jack shouted.

"No, my dear," said Madame Lucille with a sigh, "You could not."

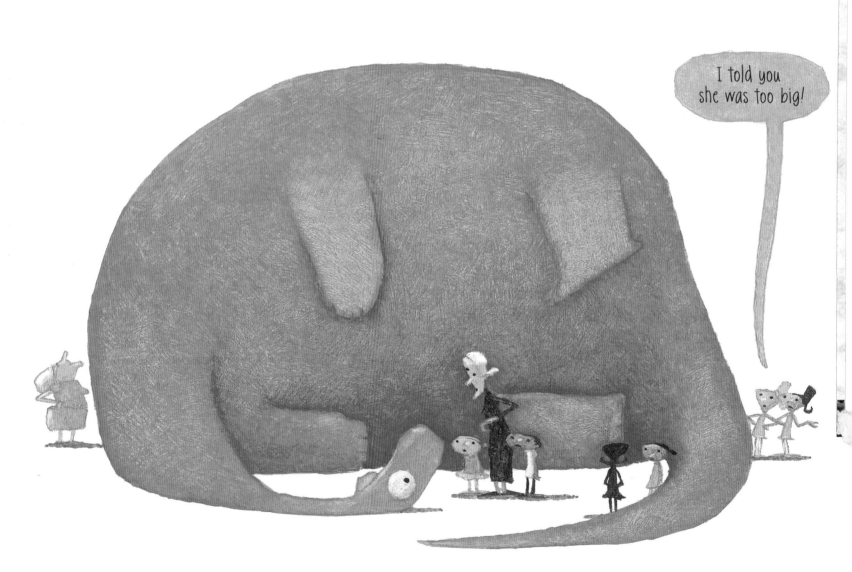

I told you she was too big!

A tear fell from Brontorina's eye.
Downcast, she turned to leave.

"Wait!" Clara called out. "Don't go. My mother has been working on a surprise for you all week, Brontorina. She is bringing it today."

"Whatever are you talking about?" Madame Lucille asked Clara.

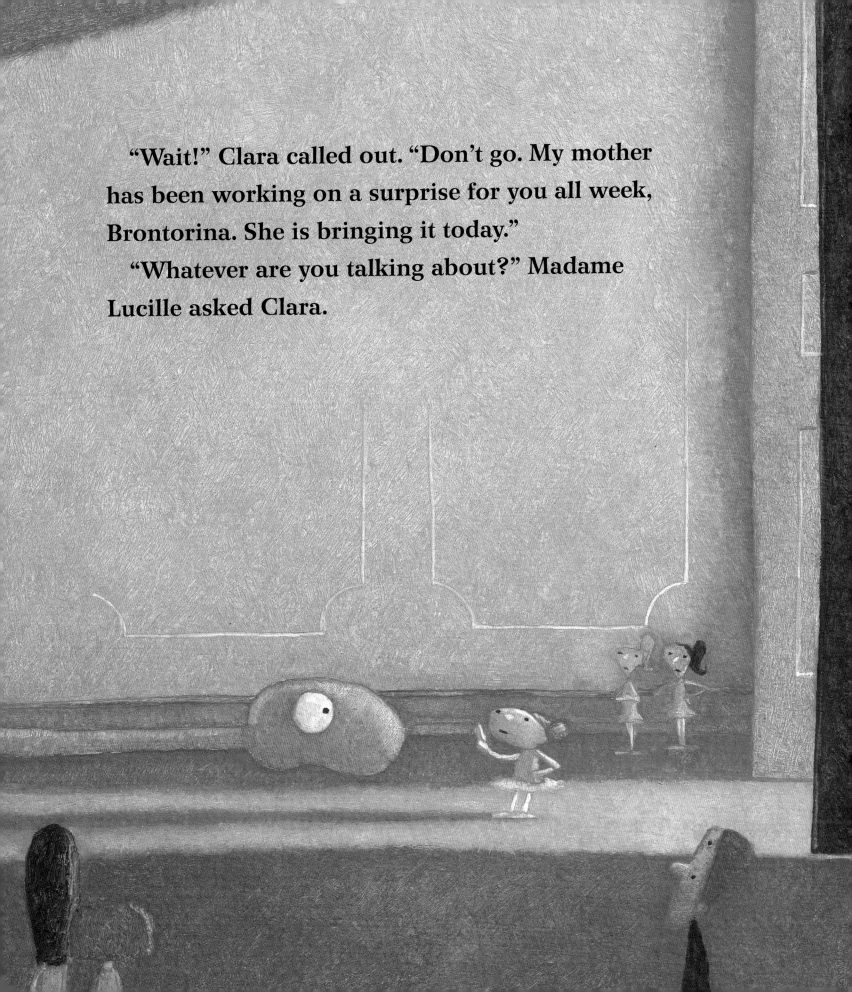

Just then, Clara's mother appeared at the door.
"You must be Brontorina," she said, holding out
the surprise. "I hope these will fit."

Well, now she has the right shoes.

Brontorina beamed. "They fit perfectly!" she cried.
"I *am* a ballerina! Or I would be . . . if only I weren't
so . . . big."

"Oh, fiddlesticks!" said Madame Lucille. "Why
didn't I see it before? The problem is not that you are
too big. The problem is that my studio is too small."

And so the whole class went off to
look for a studio big enough to hold
all of Brontorina's talent.

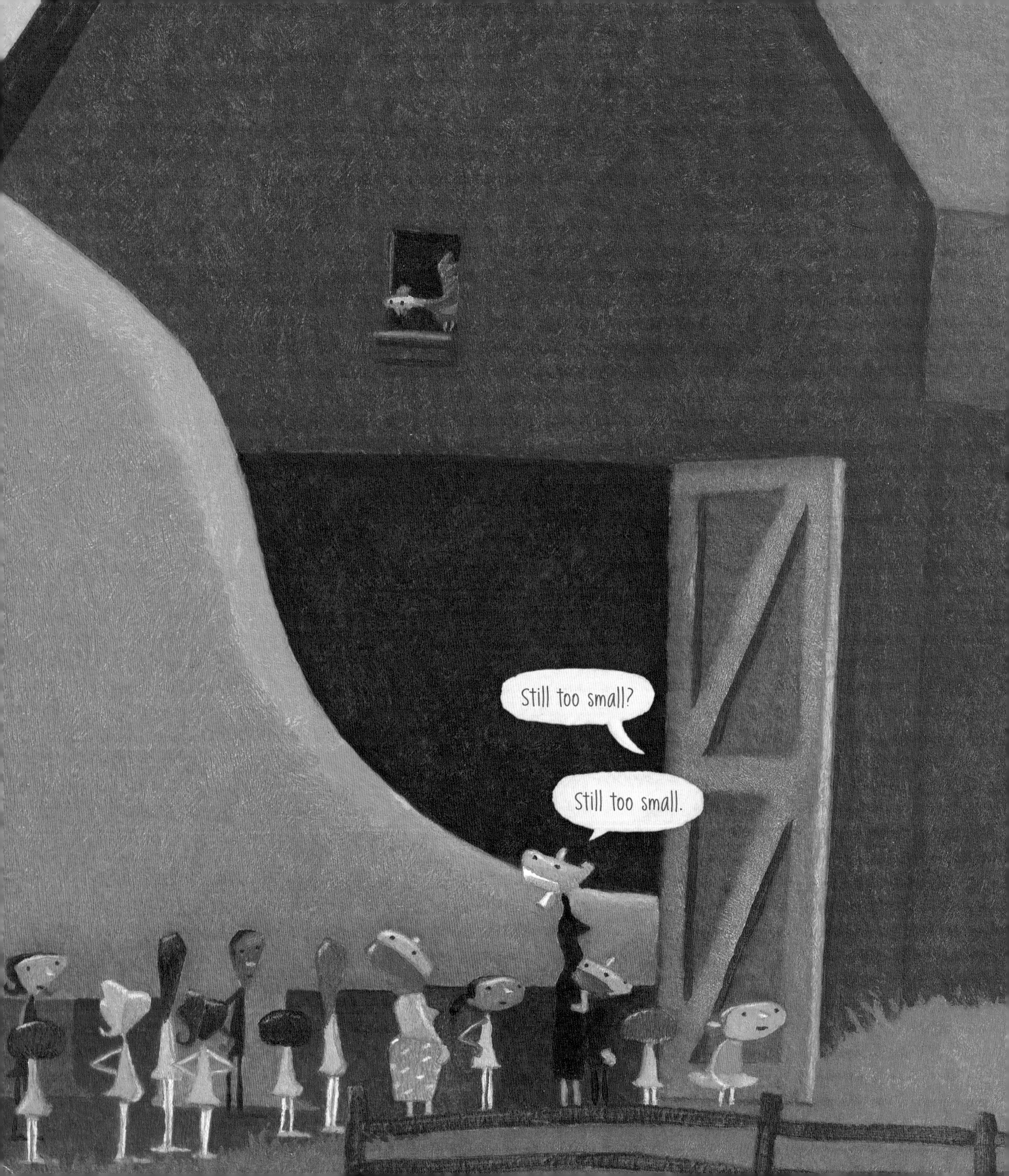
Still too small?
Still too small.

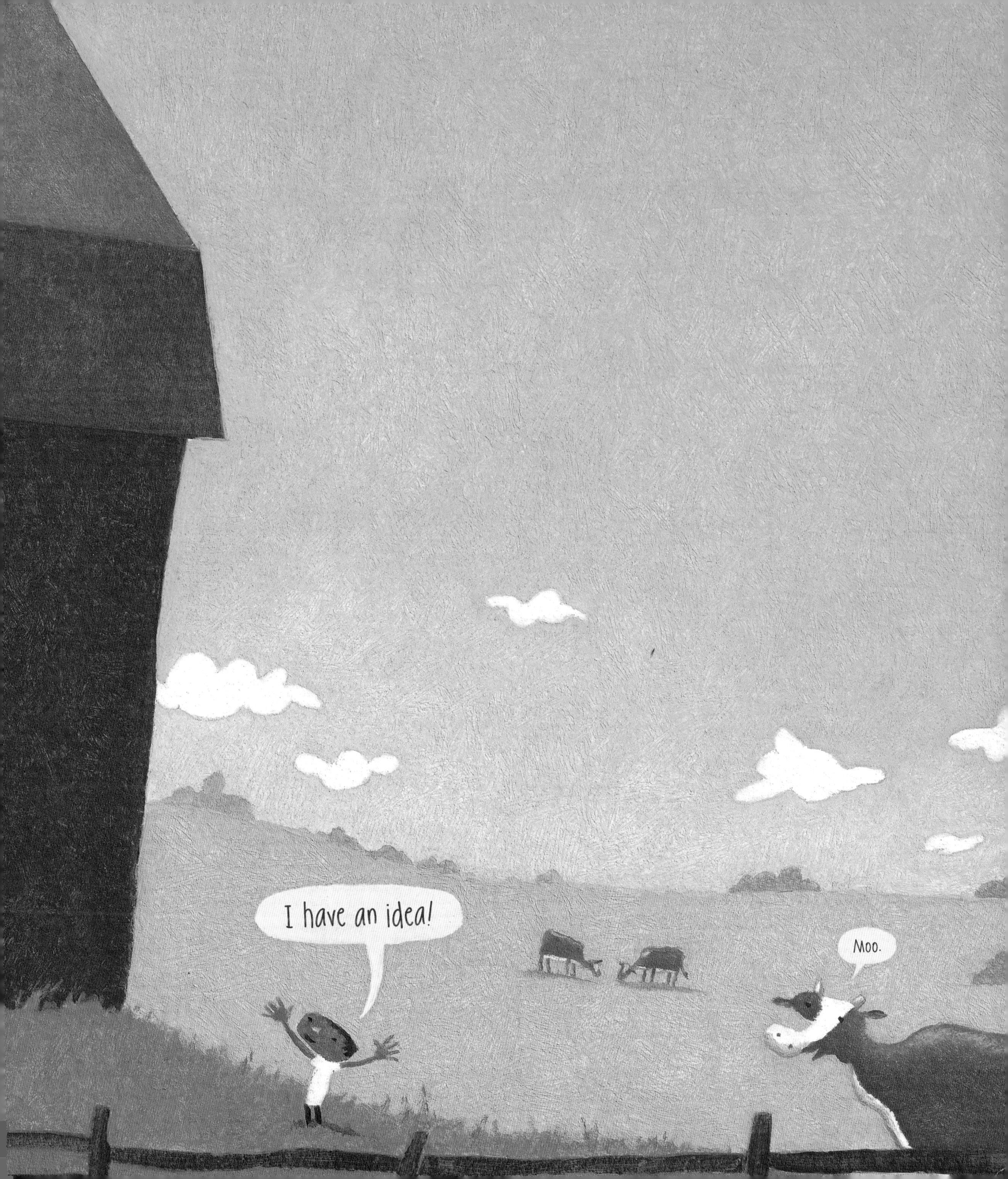
I have an idea!
Moo.

Now Madame Lucille's dance academy had room for everyone.

And it all began with a dream.